I0586967

OCEANS
Within

Elizabeth Chapman

Elizabeth Chapman

South Australia
elizabethchapmanauthor@gmail.com

© Elizabeth Chapman 2022

ISBN: 978-0-6453636-6-1

All rights reserved. Except for private study, research, criticism or reviews, as permitted under the Copyright Act, no part of this book may be reproduced, stored in a retrieval system, or transmitted in any form or by any means without prior written permission. Enquiries should be made to the author.

Author's Note: This novel is a work of fiction. Names, characters, places, and incidents are either products of the author's imagination or used fictitiously. All characters are fictional, and any similarity to people living or dead is purely coincidental.

Cataloguing-in-Publications entry is available from the National Library of Australia http:/catalogue.nla.gov.au

Second edition published 2022

For Michelle –

I will be forever grateful for your listening ear,
gentle replies, and hot coffee.

Contents

Chapter 1

Sadie dropped her phone, staring wide-eyed at her blissfully ignorant six-month-old. She briefly searched for a sign or symptom then scooped the little one up off the playmat and into her arms.

'Come on, Nyssa, let's go find the doctor...'

Nyssa's pudgy hands still clung to Molly Moo Cow. Sadie grabbed the baby bag and flung it over her other shoulder. Her heart thumped in her chest. Raking a rigid hand through her unwashed hair, she floundered for the car keys, the baby bag bouncing against her hip.

'It's okay, it's okay,' she hushed in her sing-song tone while she battled the front door of their "new" makeshift house.

If only they had done their research before accepting the job position. The fact that Vaishant even considered this position in the middle of nowhere was a testament to his priorities or lack of. Of course, he made it sound like it would be the best thing for their family and claimed it might even ease Sadie's anxiety. Little did he know, Sadie would have felt perfectly safe remaining in their house of four years if only Vaishant had been home more. Being home alone would push any new mother to the extreme.

Sadie tucked a muslin wrap over Nyssa's legs in the car seat and smoothed her bib. But why couldn't she tuck the bib in anywhere? Then it hit her with the full weight of every worst-case scenario – she hadn't buckled up the seatbelts. What if Nyssa hadn't been teething yet and Sadie decided to forgo the bib? Would she have even realised her baby was travelling sans-safety? Sadie blinked her bleary eyes. With trembling hands, she clicked the seatbelt straps into position and inhaled deeply. 'Jesus, help me.'

Sadie released a staggered breath as the car chugged down the long gravel driveway before turning onto Beach Road. What a joke. The beach was miles away Or as the landlady put it, 'Just down the road.' Sadie hadn't ventured that far yet. She was busy enough unpacking by herself and looking after a six-month-old who had started to roll and hit her head into almost everything. What would Sadie do when Nyssa decided to crawl? Or worse yet, walk! How would she cope then? She would have to watch her constantly.

When they arrived at the town medical clinic, complete with five whole carparks which were all full, Sadie pulled up to the curb and pulled the baby bag over one shoulder. As she took Nyssa from the car seat, the little one snuggled up quietly on her mother's hip. Sadie clicked the boot of the car open only to see the monstrous suitcase staring back at her. 'Of course,' she muttered. 'Your father couldn't fit the pram back in the car with his collection of books... Why he needed to bring them all when we have no place to put them...'

She continued her under-the-breath rant, only stopping when they reached the glass double doors. She then used her back to push the doors before realising the sign said *pull*. By the time she rebalanced herself, an elderly gentleman came and opened the door for her. 'Thanks,' she said then strode up to the receptionist desk and blurted, 'I think my baby may have abdominal bleeding.'

'Let me see...' the receptionist began calmly, 'I have an appointment—'

'It's an emergency!'

The receptionist glanced at a contented Nyssa, her heavy head nestled into her mother's chest, then back to Sadie. 'Just fill out this form and I'll let the doctor know you're here.'

Sadie heaved the baby bag to one side and took the clipboard she offered before adding a curt, 'Thank you.'

Chapter 2

Sadie stared at the freshly painted doorframe, forehead pressed to the cool wood, willing Vaishant to walk through the front door of the shack. It was a common practice of hers, which never actually worked.

She felt embarrassed. Mortified, really. How would she show her face at the medical clinic again? Especially after the doctor questioned her own mental state.

'She's just eaten too many bananas,' he had said.

Sadie hadn't considered the black specks could have been something so harmless and Doctor Google's diagnoses had been bleak to put it mildly. But the *real* doctor – the one with the medical degree and decades of experience – had assured her that if Nyssa *had* abdominal bleeding, she wouldn't have been as content as she was.

If only he could see her now.

Nyssa was screaming from her playmat, but Sadie couldn't bring herself to pick her up. She had tried everything already. Sadie stared harder at the white lacquered paint roughly slapped onto the wood. She had to give credit where credit was due, Vaishant's new employer had this place move in ready and fully furnished within a week. It helped that Vaishant was the only horticultural specialist willing to upend his life to join a research team in the middle of nowhere. Sadie thought it would be a new beginning for them. But she couldn't have been more wrong. Mere days in and here she was again, wondering if banging her head against the doorframe would bring relief from the anxious tension at the forefront of her mind or whether it was pure stupidity. The only thought that stopped her most days was that Nyssa needed her conscious. So, she stepped away from the odd temptation and leaned down to pick up her daughter. Instantly, the crying stopped. Tears pricked Sadie's eyes. This time at least, Nyssa just wanted her.

'Mummy's sorry...' She kissed Nyssa's sweet caramel skin, her round cheek, her button nose, her forehead. 'Mummy's sorry.'

Sadie glanced around the shack. Chaos. Unpacked boxes. Explosions of baby paraphernalia. Piles of books Vaishant assured her were important. Just as important, she supposed, as the large suitcase of books – and who knew what else – that still sat in the boot of their SUV taking up vital pram space. It was the very thing that had kept her and Nyssa at home for days on end. It was too heavy for her to lug out herself. Besides, it was the principle.

She decided she would take Nyssa for a walk. It would do them both good. Nyssa would get some fresh air and scenery and Sadie might shave a bit more off her baby body. Maybe then she would start to feel more comfortable around Vaishant again, and not like a stranger was trying to touch her.

She grabbed the baby bag and bundled Nyssa into the stroller. Pushing Nyssa with one hand, she pulled the wheely bin with the other, rattling down the long driveway. She wasn't sure when bin day was but it was already full so she figured she might as well leave it by the road. The driveway seemed a lot shorter by car. When she reached the end, she was hot and bothered, glaring up at the sun, wishing she'd thought to bring her sunglasses.

Town, she thought. We'll walk to town, I'll get a decent coffee, and hopefully Nyssa will sleep.

With two hands now steadying the stroller, she gazed down at her dark haired little six-month-old. People often asked whether Sadie had adopted, until they met Vaishant of course. Then the weirdness would continue with their preconceived racial prejudices. It was the very reason they could never decide on a church. Where Sadie felt comfortable, Vaishant felt ostracised. Where Vaishant felt accepted, Sadie couldn't connect with the other women who often slipped into their native tongue, albeit accidentally.

Once upon a time, their lives had been simple. It was them with Jesus against the world. Against expectations. Against social norms. Who would've thought such a relationship could exist between a Western white girl and a boy from the slums who her missionary mother couldn't help but sponsor? It was a lifetime ago, but Sadie would never forget her Indian summer, the year she turned ten. The next time she and Vaishant would meet in person would be at her mother's funeral eighteen years later. It was there his letters came to life, manifesting in a strong capable studious and, yes, even handsome young man.

Her mind reeled as she neared the part of the road where the dirt finally turned to bitumen and Nyssa's eyes began to grow heavy.

There wasn't a cafe as such but there was a community centre with a coffee machine by the front window. That would do.

By the time Sadie reached the counter, Nyssa was sound asleep, and Sadie released a weighted sigh. She hadn't even thought to look in the mirror before she left the shack. She tentatively patted her messy mum-bun, silently judging whether it was worth attempting a redo.

'Hi, I'm Allison. But people call me Ally.' The curly haired lady from behind the counter smiled and it touched her eyes. 'How are you?'

Sadie had been prepared to rattle off her order, but the question took her by surprise. She swallowed hard then cleared her throat. How *was* she? Couldn't they start with a less complicated question?

'I'm okay,' Sadie lied.

She mustn't have been very convincing for Ally's brow furrowed ever so slightly. 'You must be new in town,' she said lightly.

Sadie nodded then rocked the stroller for something to do.

'Well, welcome!' She churned the grinder to life. 'What can I get for you? It's on the house.'

That was all it took – a moment of kindness. Sadie's eyes filled and she muttered, 'A really big coffee and one of those... those...' She pointed.

Ally's face softened. 'Chocolate brownie?'

Sadie nodded as the tears fell.

'Hey Deb,' Ally called across the counter. 'Cover for me...'

Chapter 3

'So, Sadie, your husband is part of the new botanical research team?' Ally asked.

Sadie swallowed her mouthful of chocolate brownie as she nodded. The sweetness subdued further emotional outbursts as she sat at the café style table.

'His name is Vaishant. Maybe you've met him?'

'Tall, dark, incredibly polite and has his coffee around open at 6am?'

'Sounds like him.' Sadie liked that Ally didn't just jump straight to his nationality. Sadly, he had become used to it, just known as the "Indian guy" in most circles. But Sadie was over it.

'The early starts must be hard on your family.' Ally sipped her coffee.

'Early starts, late finishes and then I'm up half the night with her.' Sadie glanced at a sleeping Nyssa then back to Ally. 'Not that I'm not grateful. I always wanted to be a mum. I just didn't think it would happen so quickly

I suppose. We had only been married a few months when we found out and...' She shook her head. 'I don't know why I'm telling you all this.'

Ally leaned closer from across the table. 'Sounds like you need to tell somebody.'

Sadie smiled weakly. 'I'm so blessed... I should be more grateful.'

Ally took her hand. 'You can be grateful and still admit when things are hard. Motherhood is tough. Nothing prepares you for it. And it's okay. Whatever you're feeling, it's all okay. You just need to know when it becomes too much. And then you need to ask for help.'

Sadie ate the last mouthful of brownie then washed it down with coffee. 'I should get Nyssa home. She'll be due for a bottle soon.'

'Why don't you come by again tomorrow,' Ally said. 'We can continue our little chat. Same time?'

Before Sadie could consider her response, Ally held out a card.

'Here's my number if you need *anything.*'

Later in the afternoon, once Sadie promised to return to the community centre the following day, she and Nyssa played in the shallow apricot-enamel tub of the shack's small bathroom. She had measured the temperature of the water at a perfect 37.5 degrees Celsius, so she knew they didn't have long before it started to turn cold. Still, Nyssa splashed and washed off the day, the dusty road and leftover mashed banana and sweet potato.

Sadie's hands never left Nyssa's underarms. Bathing her on her own was awkward but she figured a rinse off was better than no bath at all.

Then Sadie heard a noise. She was certain it was the front door. But she had locked it, hadn't she? She glanced down at their vulnerable bodies then to the towel laden laundry basket beside the bath. Could she quickly put Nyssa in there and reach the phone in time? Who would she call? 000? Ally?

Her heart thumped hard in her chest until it was all she could hear.

'Sshh,' she hushed Nyssa, silently hoping not to draw attention to themselves. The intruder could come and go, take whatever they wanted. Just not Nyssa. She had heard the news stories over the years, children who had gone missing...

Why did they have to move to a remote community? And on the outskirts of the town...

'Jesus,' she whispered in desperation, 'protect us...'

When the bathroom door swung open, Sadie screamed. Nyssa cried. And Vaishant stood wide eyed.

Sadie clutched Nyssa to her bare chest and swiped her three-day-old mascara from her eyes. 'You're *early!*'

Vaishant knelt by the bath, placing a gentle hand on Sadie's naked back. She flinched.

'I'm sorry,' he said, 'I thought it would be a nice surprise. I should have called.'

Sadie's heartbeat began to steady, and Nyssa relaxed in her arms enough to wiggle around, hands outstretched for her daddy.

'My little Princess Nyssie.' He smiled and took her wet body.

'Careful,' Sadie muttered.

For a flickering moment, Vaishant looked at his wife. An old familiar glint in his eye. Or had she imagined it? Vaishant didn't want her that way anymore. Not since the baby. Maybe it was the pregnancy and seeing her grow as big as the tub she now sat in. Naked. Vulnerable. Maybe it was seeing her writhing and bloodied in the delivery room. Or maybe it was the stripes that now scared her body, the extra love handles, the parts of her that never bounced back. She may have squeezed into her old jeans but nothing could permanently flatten the post-partum pouch she sported.

'Are you getting out?' Vaishant asked.

Sadie curled her knees to her chest. 'In a minute.'

Once Vaishant carried Nyssa out of the bathroom, Sadie quickly dried and put on her tracksuit bottoms and favourite frumpy concert t-shirt – so faded she couldn't even remember the band. She then knotted her brassy hair up in another bun. One day she would get to washing it. One day.

She went to the kitchen to see Nyssa sitting happily in her Bumbo on the kitchen bench while Vaishant searched the fridge.

'I thought I'd cook dinner,' he said.

Sadie glanced at a potted green stalk by the window overlooking their wilderness of a backyard. 'What's this?

'A rare orchid that has been discovered here,' Vaishant said as he retrieved a bunch of vegetables from the crisper. 'We're waiting for them to bloom again. I thought you might like it.'

'What do I have to do to it?'

'Nothing.' He grinned at her the way he used to and for the briefest moment she felt a foreign flutter. 'It'll just about take care of itself.'

Sadie sighed. Good. The last thing she needed was another mouth to feed. Particularly since she was such a terrible cook.

Vaishant whipped together his mildest curry recipe, steamed the coconut rice to perfection, corked a bottle of white wine, and even placed Nyssa's highchair beside him so he could spoon-feed her.

'Wine? What's the occasion?' Sadie asked.

'I've been offered a permanent position with the horticultural centre once the research is complete.' Vaishant looked over at Sadie, searching for a reaction.

She poured herself a glass of Chardonnay. 'That's great.'

Witching hour then came on cue and sapped all that remained of Sadie's patience. By the time dinner was done and Nyssa was down in her cot, Sadie was once again hot and bothered. She retreated to the couch for a second glass of wine.

'So how was your day?' Vaishant asked, settling in beside her.

She took a sip. 'Long. But we walked to the community centre, that was nice.'

'Walked?'

Sadie wanted to rant an explanation, but a small sensible voice reminded her that not only had Vaishant been working all day in the sun, but he also cooked dinner for them, brought her a stem – which might be a flower one day – and wine.

'We might do it again tomorrow.'

'I like that place,' he said, gazing off for a moment. 'You know they run a church service on Sundays.'

'No, Ally didn't mention it.'

'She probably didn't want to assume.'

Sadie nodded.

'Hey,' Vaishant said gently, placing his hand on her knee as she perched on the couch cross-legged.

Again, she flinched.

This time he kept his hand there. 'I'm sorry for startling you earlier. Are you okay?'

Just as Sadie was about to give her husband an honest answer, Nyssa began to cry in the other room. She shrugged and unfolded herself from the couch.

By the time Sadie returned, still holding a sleeping Nyssa, Vaishant had fallen asleep on the couch. So, Sadie carried her little one to their bed where she could sleep close and watch her breathe. When Vaishant eventually woke and came to bed, Sadie pretended to be asleep. She waited for the rustling of quilts to hush while he settled into their bed, and then she listened. She listened for the creaks of the shack, for the sounds of nature that surrounded them. She listened for anything out of the ordinary. Anytime Vaishant would stir in his sleep, she started, listening again to be sure that's all it was. Nothing more. Nothing sinister. September weather could be unpredictable, and even in their bedroom she could hear the light rain and a subtle breeze.

Suddenly, Sadie leapt out of bed over an unfamiliar sound. She switched on the hallway light, pacing the length of the shack. Her imagination conjured scenarios of intruders, so she dutifully checked all the windows and doors for a third time. When she eventually went to the bathroom to splash her face, her anxious self was certain she would see a second face staring back at her in the mirror, like in one of those old horror films. So, she kept her eyes closed and buried in the towel. Here, she began to sob. Her knees buckled beneath her, and she curled up on the bathroom floor, crying.

'Hey, what's going on?' Vaishant was at her side, holding her. 'You're shaking.'

'I thought I heard a noise...'

Vaishant pulled her onto him.

'Nyssa,' Sadie panicked, pulling away from him.

But he wasn't having it. 'I've put pillows around her, she's fine... Sadie, I thought this had stopped?'

Her body began to relax within the warmth of his arms. 'So did I.'

Chapter 4

Sadie roused from another restless sleep, unsure of whether she had even slept. The night's noises had been relentless and when she wasn't keenly listening, her eyes were staring with laser focus watching in the dim glow of the nightlight to make sure Nyssa's chest was rising and falling the way it should. Finally, around 4am, Vaishant propped up in bed to read the Bible app on his phone while Nyssa slept soundly beside him. In this groggy hour before he had to get ready for work, Sadie finally went for a shower to wash her knotted oily hair. She had to use the conditioner first just to make the shampoo workable. But as the hot water poured over her body, she felt herself relax. Nyssa was safe. Vaishant was there. For these few moments, she could just breathe. She lathered, scrubbed and rinsed countless times, indulging in the rarity of this moment. The water bordered on scalding, just the way she liked it. And in this quiet moment, when the anxiety of the night had finally loosened its grip on her, the faintest whisper in her heart reminded her – '*I have not given you a Spirit of fear, but of love, power, and self-control.*'

Her hands fell to her cheeks. Water fell like rain over her. She began to wonder when was the last time she spoke those words over herself. Certainly not since the move.

It had been her lifeline three months ago when she had spoken to her therapist. Then the job opportunity happened and life became complicated again and Sadie once again lost sense of who she was.

'You are a child of God,' the therapist had told her.

She didn't feel like one. She felt like a failure of a mother, a wife who couldn't even be attractive for her husband, and a singer-songwriter who never picked up a pencil or played a single note. She didn't even own a piano anymore. Who was she without it? She didn't know anymore.

Once her skin was both fresh and set ablaze by the heat, she dried off and wrapped her large dressing gown about herself then marched barefoot back to the bedroom. How did Vaishant look so good first thing in the morning? Men had it so easy.

She perched on his side of the bed and whispered, 'We should go to the community church on Sunday.'

He began to nod. 'I was thinking the same thing.'

Sadie pressed her tongue to the roof of her mouth, her eyes rolling toward the ceiling as they filled. 'I don't want to be this way,' she confessed. 'I'm so... so tired...'

Vaishant put his phone down on the bedside table and gazed at her. Tentatively, he rested his hand on her bare knee. 'I don't have to leave for a while still. Why don't you go have a cup of coffee? There's my old Bible on the dining table.'

Sadie slowly nodded before drifting back to the hallway.

'And Sadie,' Vaishant whispered as she reached the doorway.

'Hmm?'

'I love you.'

Tears rolled down her cheeks as she nodded, unable to speak, then she made her way to the quiet kitchen. There was something about knowing Vaishant was not only home but awake that comforted her. His snoring at night only kept her awake, not because of the noise but because she felt the need to be alert, to protect her family, to hear anything that threatened them. Now, the morning was quiet, and so was the storm inside of her.

She made herself a strong instant coffee – the only kind she had the patience to make for herself these days – and then sat down at the dining table. She opened the stained tattered copy of God's Word to one of its many bookmarks. This one had a cartoon of Jesus standing in the boat of his disciples silencing the waves. She knew it well. Her mother had made them for the children she visited over the years. It was no wonder Vaishant's childhood Bible was filled with them.

'A furious squall came up, and the waves broke over the boat, so that it was nearly swamped. Jesus was in the stern, sleeping on a cushion. The disciples woke him and said to him, "Teacher, don't you care if we drown?" He got up, rebuked the wind and said to the waves, "Quiet! Be still!" Then the wind died down and it was completely calm. He said to his disciples, "Why are you so afraid? Do you still have no faith?" Mark 4:37-40

'Why are you afraid? Do you still have no faith?'

The words shook Sadie to her core. After everything they had been through. After everything she had seen through her mother's ministry. After defying all odds and expectations and visas and nationalisation, she now had the audacity to doubt God's faithfulness to her? To her family?

She tore back through the pages, landing in Matthew...

'Do not be afraid of those who kill the body but cannot kill the soul. Rather, be afraid of the One who can destroy both soul and body in hell. Are not two sparrows sold for a penny? Yet not one of them will fall to the ground outside your Father's care. And even the very hairs of your head are all numbered. So don't be afraid; you are worth more than many sparrows.' Matthew 10:28-31

'Jesus,' she whispered. 'Help me...'

Chapter 5

When Sadie arrived at the community centre later that afternoon, Nyssa was asleep and Ally was ready with two takeaway lattes and a brown paper bag.

'I thought we could walk down to the water,' she said with a bright smile.

Sadie didn't have the heart to tell her she was already exhausted, and that she would have energy if only her husband had just moved that suitcase as he said he was going to. Two cars and a removal van and it had to be *her* car that dead weight had been left in.

'Sounds great,' Sadie lied as best as she could.

'Here.' Ally handed her the coffee. 'You get started, I'll push the stroller.'

Sadie almost politely declined but the offer was too good. So, she took the coffees, and sipped from the cup with a scrawled black "S" and smiley face on the lid.

'How did you sleep?' Ally asked.

'Terrible. I kept hearing noises.'

'And what happens when you hear the noises?'

'I lay awake listening to make sure it isn't something dangerous, I want to know where the noise is coming from.'

Ally slowly nodded as she pushed the stroller. 'Something dangerous, like...'

'Someone breaking into the shack.'

'Have you had a break in before?'

Sadie sipped her coffee. 'Yeah, in our old house. A racist local. They graphited our loungeroom because they assumed Vaishant was some sort of terrorist.'

Ally stopped. 'Sadie, that's terrifying.'

'Yeah. I thought I had dealt with it. Then Nyssa came along, and all those fears came back. What if she had been there?'

'Regardless of whether you had Nyssa or not, that is still an absolutely awful situation, and you are completely justified to be shaken by it. Just *you*. It's okay to be afraid. It's just not okay to stay afraid and dwell in fear.'

Ally started pushing the stroller again, down to where the bitumen thinned to sand, and the sound of the waves travelled over the crest of long yellow grass. She then pushed it onto the sandy crest – not an easy feat, but Sadie didn't argue – and then stopped there. Ally clicked the brake and sat down beside the stroller.

'You've done this before.' Sadie smiled and sat down.

'Only every day through those early years. My three are teenagers now but you never forget this stage. Ever. It's both precious and exhausting.'

Sadie was still overwhelmed by the word - 'Three?'

'Oh, you forget enough of the exhaustion to go back and do it again.'

'I think one might be enough for us.'

'Give yourself time. Time to heal. Time to enjoy her, *just* her.'

'How is it, in motherhood, you can you have so much joy and yet so much fear at once?' Sadie asked.

'It doesn't have to be that way,' Ally said gently. 'I remember I was a mess with my first. I ended up on medication just to help with the anxiety.'

'What changed?'

'It was pretty simple actually, I was reminded that God didn't give me a Spirit of fear but power, love, and a sound mind. I didn't feel like I had a very sound mind at the time. So I just pressed into Jesus. When the CBT didn't work, I saturated myself in the Word of God. I wrote verses on post-it notes and put them in the kitchen and the bathroom, even above the change table! I wanted a sound mind and as much as I believe in the power of medicine, I needed *more*. I needed to heal deeply. Rip the root out, not just the weed.'

'I spoke to a therapist a few months ago who said the same thing.'

Ally took a gulp of coffee. 'And?'

'And I haven't been using my Cognitive Behavioural Therapy techniques, but they did help when I used to. And I read the Bible this morning for the first time in I don't know how long.'

'And how do you feel?'

'Honestly? Like the biggest failure. I'm failing at my marriage, motherhood, and I'm failing God.'

'Why do you feel like you're failing in your marriage?'

Sadie's eyes glazed over. 'We're like ships passing in the night. We were closer when we were an ocean apart trying to be together. Now, it's like everything we fought for is gone.'

'It's not gone,' Ally said, handing her a piece of chocolate brownie wrapped in a napkin. 'It's all well and good to have that passion before marriage, but now you need to fight to keep it.'

'I don't even know where to start '

'Start by being in God's Word every single morning, no matter how difficult.'

Sadie nodded. 'I can do that.' Or at least, she wanted to believe she could.

'And come to the community centre on an afternoon, and we can come here for a chat.'

'Don't you have things to do?'

'Sadie, did you even read my business card? This *is* what I do.'

'Hmm?'

'I'm a counsellor at the community centre. It's a government incentive. And they've been encouraging me to do more one-on-one meetings and to let the other staff members cover the cafe, but I haven't found the need. Until I met you.'

'I guess few people are as messed up as me,' Sadie breathed.

'Uh-uh. Few people are as *brave* as you to admit they need help.'

'I don't feel very brave right now.'

'Hon, you have no idea how much courage is needed to admit where you're at isn't where you want to be. So, same time tomorrow?'

Sadie nodded. 'But will you at least let me buy my own coffee?'

'Not a chance.' She grinned. 'Just let me bless you, okay?'

Chapter 6

'How did we sleep?' Ally chimed as Sadie walked through the front door of the community centre the following day.

'Better.' Sadie breathed a sigh of relief. 'In fact, I was wondering, rather than the beach, whether the horticultural site is walking distance?'

'Sure, it is. Coffee's ready, let's go.'

A cooler afternoon greeted them. Ally once again took the stroller, giving Sadie a break. As they walked, Sadie told Ally about her quiet time in Psalm 127 and that God said he give his beloved sleep. 'And he gave me sleep last night, a whole five hours.'

'Well, you got to take what you can get, that's for sure.' Ally grinned. 'So why the sudden urge to see the site?'

'I'm curious. I want to see where Vaishant spends all his time. I feel like, if I'm going to work through all this and move forward, we can't keep living separate lives. I should know where he works at least. So, I can connect on some level when he gets home.'

'Again, bravery, my friend,' Ally said. 'It's not easy to step out of your comfort zone but you're doing it.'

Sadie didn't realise the amount of courage it would take to approach her husband when they arrived. For there in the middle of an ornate glass house surrounded by orchids stood her Vaishant in a matching uniform to the slim brunette sporting a bright smile and a small pair of shears. Sadie might have slipped back out the way she came had Vaishant not seen her.

'Sadie!' There was no shame in his voice only sheer joy. 'Jo, come and meet my wife,' he said proudly.

Jo? Sadie had assumed his employer was a male. Had he deliberately not told her? Maybe he didn't want to make her concerned. Still, the way he strode over to her, kissing Sadie's hair, and nestling his hand possessively on her hip, told her otherwise.

Part of her wanted to be angry at him, to punish him for not being honest at least how pretty and young and, well, *female* his employer actually was. But then, there was his hand on her. And she hadn't even flinched. He held a determined grasp, one that clearly stated this woman was his wife. And for the first time in a long time, Sadie felt grateful.

'It's nice to meet you, Jo,' Sadie managed.

'Likewise, I've heard so much about you. And little Nyssie, of course. Is she awake? I love babies.'

Nyssie? Frustration began to boil again. 'Sorry, she's sleeping.'

'Nice to see you again, Ally,' Vaishant said.

Sadie wasn't sure if he was purposely changing the subject. Either way, she was grateful this picture-perfect horticulturalist wouldn't be holding their Nyssie.

'How has she been?' Vaishant asked, gazing down into Sadie's eyes.

She had almost forgotten how tall he was. A full head above her, he leaned in close. Intimately. His fathomless brown eyes searching her pale grey ones.

'Good,' Sadie said quietly. 'These walks have been perfect. She falls asleep halfway down the dirt road and just about stays asleep till she's due for her next bottle.'

'And Mama gets a coffee and a brownie and a well-deserved break,' Ally added.

'Well, yeah.'

Vaishant gave Sadie a little squeeze. 'Brownie, hey. Where's mine?'

Sadie half-smiled. 'Next time.'

'In that case, I should really get back to work.'

'This place is really beautiful,' Sadie said. 'I'm glad we came by.'

'So am I,' Vaishant said, kissing her cheek. He then peered into the stroller. 'Sure I can't wake her?'

Sadie's eyes narrowed.

'Kidding.' He smirked and held up his palms. 'I wouldn't dare. Love you,' he called as he lightly jogged back to his station of unflowering stalks.

Sadie smiled to herself as they left the glass house and emerged onto the sunny patio.

'Well, I don't think you're failing at marriage as much as you think.' Ally giggled. 'I haven't seen a man that besotted with a woman since I don't know when.'

'Besotted?'

'A-ha, and don't you forget it.'

Sadie sipped her coffee as they walked. *Besotted? Vaishant?* The last time someone had used that word, Sadie was ten years old and Vaishant had just promised to marry her when he grew up.

Chapter 7

Sunlight pierced the gap in the curtains, stirring Sadie awake. Squinting and stretching, she rolled over to see empty sheets. Panic set in. She threw back the quilt, scouted the floor then ran barefoot to the lounge. There, Nyssa was nestled into her daddy's arms drinking her bottle.

Sadie exhaled and focused on her heartbeat wild in her chest.

'I thought you could do with a sleep-in,' Vaishant said.

'Why, what day is it?'

'Saturday.'

She nodded slowly before drifting over to them. She placed a kiss on Nyssa's chubby cheek. Then, before she could escape, Vaishant caught her hand and pulled her in, planting a kiss straight on her mouth.

'Good morning.'

'Morning,' she breathed as she made her way to the kitchen. Two takeaway coffee cups sat on the dining table. 'Where did these come from?'

'I drove Nyssa down to the community centre this morning.'

Sadie looked at the microwave clock. 8am. She hadn't slept this late since her second trimester between the months of turbulent morning sickness and the later elephant syndrome. Still, he took their daughter for a drive without her knowledge.

'Did you at least leave a note? What if I had woken up to find her missing?'

'Well, she wasn't missing, she was with me.'

'I wouldn't know that.' Sadie's voice escalated. 'I barely know what day it is I'm so stuck in this world of nappies and bottles and crying...' Her own floodgates opened. 'Did you even *consider* that?'

Vaishant rose, still holding Nyssa. He pecked Sadie's forehead then calmly said, 'Enjoy your coffee. I'm going to take Nyssa for a drive.'

Sadie stood dumbfounded. Seething. Why? He had tried to do something nice, and she was throwing it in his face.

He took the baby bag and Sadie's car keys from the hook by the door. 'My car is still out there if you need it.'

Then he left.

No 'I love you'.

Just a cool exit.

Sadie glanced at the table. He hadn't even taken his coffee.

She flipped open the laptop and began to gulp her caffeine down as though her life depended on it. She then searched for the online test* she had done all those months ago, when she first felt like something was wrong.

Tired for no reason? Tick. Nervous? Tick. Feeling hopeless? Tick. What about restless? Tick.

Depressed... Tick.

Feel worthless... Tick. Always.

Her score was higher now than when she had been only three months postpartum and ended up in therapy. She would call it 'counselling' but really, she was seeing a therapist. Only, she didn't like that word.

Now she could say she was speaking to a counsellor, but had she even really opened up to Ally? Was she holding back for fear of being judged? Would her dark thoughts forever discredit her from being a healthy and godly wife and mother? She felt like she was attempting the impossible. It was too hard. And yet, not for one moment did she think Nyssa was better off without her. That was what she typically thought postpartum depression looked like. No, Sadie had the opposite problem. She didn't believe anyone else could take care of Nyssa like she could. Not even her own father.

'Oh, Vaishant...'

Did he ever regret marrying her? She didn't even feel like the same person anymore. Surely, he felt the

31

same. Who was this strange woman who shared his bed but not his life? Who took care of their child but had seemed to lose interest in him? Of course, she hadn't lost interest. Not in the least. But there were aspects of her now she didn't like, and she assumed he wouldn't like them either. Why would he want to make love to a woman so vastly changed? When they met, she was vibrant, young, and happy. When they reunited at her mother's funeral, even in grief she smiled at him, held him, mourned with him, and loved him. Now, she didn't know how to love him. Or even just how to take one step toward him.

Now, alone, Sadie didn't know what to do with herself. So, she cleaned. She wiped surfaces, dusted, sorted Vaishant's books by colour across the built-ins, and then began to steam vegetables for baby food. Anything to keep her hands busy and her mind occupied. As the morning went on, however, an unsettling grew in her heart. What if something happened to them? She shook her head and brought logic into her headspace. The likelihood was low, therefore, according to her therapist, this was an illegitimate fear, not an authentic one. This was her postpartum anxiety speaking. Vaishant was a safe driver. Nyssa was good in the car and usually slept. The two of them would be fine.

After a long hot shower, Sadie made a cup of tea and stared out into the backyard. It would be nice if Nyssa could play out there one day. Now it looked like a jungle and even she wouldn't endeavour out there. It was then

Sadie noticed the smallest bud forming on her stem by the window. It was so small it could've been missed entirely but sure enough, there it was.

New growth.

Sadie flinched at a knock on the front door. The same front door she pressed her head against daily willing the tension in her mind to subside and her gratefulness to flourish. Somehow though, she never managed to completely get passed the mental barrier. There was always something pulling her back to that dark headspace, kicking and screaming. Or rather, often, a screaming baby and an endless to-do list. Now that she was catching up on house things, would she feel any better?

She opened the front door to see Ally on the porch. She swiftly pushed aside the vision of police officers that so often plagued her mind, officers sent to tell her bad news. It had never happened, of course. Only in the movies as far as Sadie's experience went. Still, there could be a first for everything.

'Oh, hi, I wasn't expecting you. Come in...'

Ally's feet remained planted outside. 'Sadie,' she said gently, 'I need you to come with me. There has been an accident.'

Sadie felt the blood drain from her face as her hands trembled. 'What do you mean? You're not the police...'

Ally's brow furrowed. 'Sadie, honey, come with me and I'll explain on the way to the hospital.'

'Oh, Jesus, no.' Sadie's knees buckled beneath her and Ally caught her just in time.

'Nyssa is okay,' Ally said firmly. 'She's okay.'

Sadie's heart thudded in her chest. Her ears. Everywhere. It took over her entire being as she drank in the words. She's okay. She's okay. Then, the realisation struck her like lightning. 'Vaishant...'

Ally didn't answer but her face twisted into a look Sadie had never seen before. 'He's... he's not so good, hon.'

Gasping for breath, Sadie was led to the car. Ally helped her in, securing the seat belt. As they drove, Ally's words brought Sadie's worst nightmare to life.

'He was driving down the highway, back to town from the Roadhouse. He stopped at an intersection but someone didn't brake in time and went up the back of him... and then he hit the car in front... I'm so sorry, Sadie. For some reason he was sitting so far forward and his head hit the windscreen...'

The words hit her like an oncoming train. 'He didn't want to change the car seat.' Sadie sobbed. 'Because I complain when he messes with my... with my... my...'

Ally kept one hand on the wheel and clutched Sadie's knee with the other. 'Jesus, we ask for your peace over this precious family and we pray for healing in Your Name. In the powerful name of Jesus Christ, we pray for healing over this family. Over Vaishant. Over Sadie. Over Nyssa. May this strengthen them, Lord, as they seek You. In Jesus' name...'

Ally prayed all the way to the hospital.

'My husband's the Sargent, by the way,' Ally said quietly. 'That's how I knew...'

Sadie dumbly nodded. 'I just want to see my family.'

Through sterile corridors, Sadie was led to a flicker of colour. A nursery where Nyssa clung to a woollen trauma bear while nestled on the paediatrician's lap.

Sadie ran to her, and Nyssa reached for her mummy. 'Thank you, Jesus,' Sadie breathed.

'I'm Dr Lindsay,' the paediatrician said quietly, 'your daughter is fine, Mrs Patel. Better than fine. She slept through the whole ordeal.'

Sadie stared at him with wide bleary eyes as she held her daughter to her chest. 'How is that even possible?'

'It's a miracle, actually,' Ally said. 'Do you know there's a big old suitcase in the boot of your car? Apparently, it absorbed a lot of the impact.'

Sadie glanced from Ally to the paediatrician, then to the Sargent lingering in the doorway. 'Please,' she whispered, kissing Nyssa's dark hair, 'I need to see my husband.'

'How about I stay here with little Nyssa then,' Ally said in a sing-song voice.

Sadie nodded as the Sargent stepped aside from the doorway. 'This way, Sadie. I'm Keith, Ally's husband.'

All Sadie could do was nod. This wasn't the time for pleasantries. She needed to see Vaishant.

'I'm sorry to say the car is a write-off,' he explained as they walked. 'The suitcase, however, is still intact. I'll be sure to get that to you later today.'

Sadie nodded. The words blurred together. So did the halls. Part of her wanted to be anxious for Nyssa but miraculously, she was fine. And Ally was there. And a paediatrician. She was fine. Praise Jesus, she was fine. Nyssa didn't need her right now. Vaishant did.

Keith led Sadie through the intensive care ward. She tried not to hear the excruciating moans from the other beds. He stopped by a blue curtain and said softly, 'I'll let the doctor know you're here.'

With trembling hands, Sadie drew back the curtain. Bandages wrapped around Vaishant's head, and his closed eyes were black and blue. She went to his side in an instant, reaching for his bandaged hand.

'Mrs Patel?'

Sadie looked up, staring at the doctor.

'I'm Dr Robinson. Your husband has sustained a significant head injury. We are just waiting on the MRI and CT scan results to see if he will need surgery.'

Sadie's breath caught in her chest. 'Brain surgery?'

'His lack of responses show that there may be some internal bleeding, but we aren't sure as yet.'

Sadie tentatively kissed Vaishant's hand. 'I'm so sorry... this is all my fault...'

Chapter 8

Early the following morning, Ally was on Sadie's front porch with coffee, muffins and chocolate brownies. 'I can watch Nyssa,' she said. 'Will you be okay to drive yourself to the hospital?'

'Yes, of course.' Sadie made her way back to the loungeroom where Nyssa gnawed on a rusk in her highchair. 'Mummy loves you so much, sweetheart.' She kissed Nyssa's forehead, cheek, and nose.

'So, this is the miracle worker, hey?' Ally said, staring down the massive suitcase. 'What's even in there?'

Sadie sighed. 'I hadn't even thought to check.' After a sip of coffee, she eased the suitcase into its side and battled the zip. It was full, that was for sure, bulging with hardcover textbooks. However, as she began to shift the books, there beneath them were piles of envelopes. She held her breath.

'What is it?' Ally asked. 'What's wrong?'

Sadie carefully took out one of the envelopes addressed to Vaishant Patel via the ministry her mother used to run. 'My letters... these are my letters to him...' Tears stung her eyes. 'All of them.'

Hastily, she removed the weight of the books then collected the letters together, filling five shopping bags. She then stepped back to look at them. Appreciating the legacy standing before her. One letter had floated to the ground, she retrieved it instantly. The address was different. It was Vaishant's old apartment when he began working and supporting himself and his family. She eased it open, unfolding the letter written by her own hand.

Dear Vaishant,

I miss you. I think about you all the time. I know this is probably forward and not what women in your culture do, but I know what I want.

I want you.

All those years ago you asked me to marry you. You were so polite and gentlemanly when we met again at Mum's funeral but I know you felt something too. I could feel it when you hugged me.

I know you're too polite now to make the first move, so I'm going to put myself out there and risk making a fool of myself.

I wanted to kiss you after dinner, when we said goodnight and goodbye. Twenty-four hours was never going to be long enough.

I know it's complicated. I know you have your family to support and you have a life in India. But I can't stop thinking about you.

If you feel the same, I will be on the next plane to wherever you are.

I loved you the moment I met you and I still love you now.

Love, your Sadie

'Wow,' Ally gasped. 'I'm blushing!'

'Tell me about it...' Sadie felt the heat rise to her own cheeks as she remembered penning the letter, her desire for him and him alone.

'So, what happened?' Ally asked, starry-eyed.

'As soon as he received the letter, he booked a flight and came back to me.' Sadie smiled to herself. 'And proposed – *again* – when I met him at the airport.'

'What a whirlwind.'

Sadie slipped a second page from behind the letter.

'Dare I ask what *that* is?'

'A love song,' Sadie said. 'I wrote him a song.'

'I didn't know you were a songwriter?'

'I used to be,' Sadie said quietly and collected a few more of the letters. 'I better go.'

'Yes, go, we'll be fine.'

Sadie nodded and smiled. 'I'm sorry, I just realised you're missing church.'

'Well, I look forward to another Sunday when we can all go together.'

Sadie planted another kiss, or three, on Nyssa before driving to the hospital armed with coffee, snacks, and reading material. When she arrived, she discovered Vaishant had been moved to a ward. There was no internal bleeding. *Thank you, Jesus...*

'Hi baby.' Sadie leaned over and softly pecked his cheek. She then nestled into the chair beside him and placed her hand on his. 'Ally is watching Nyssa. She's okay. More than okay. That suitcase of yours protected her, can you believe it?' She released a breathy laugh and leaned in close. 'But now you have to get better. Okay? Because I have a lot of making up to do and it's hard to do when you're in a hospital bed.' She rested her head on his arm and sighed. 'I found the letters. All of them. I can't believe you kept them all this time... Please wake up, Shan. I need you. And Nyssie needs you. Please... please wake up...'

After almost falling asleep herself, Sadie grabbed another coffee and took a stroll around the hospital to clear her head. Nyssa was fine. According to Ally's last text, she was napping. Vaishant was still unconscious, but his responses were improving. In all Sadie's wandering, she eventually found herself in a small inner chapel, a sanctuary of warmth and comfort in amongst the clinical surroundings. And there, by the ornate cross where countless had no doubt committed their loved ones in prayer, stood an upright piano. She pulled a pen from her bag and one of the envelopes and rested them on the music stand. Then, like a novice, she found middle C. Slowly, her fingers found their way back home, stumbling over a few coarse notes before finding a little melody Sadie could once again call her own.

Here I am, on my knees
Begging Jesus, please, rescue me

Calm the storm that rages on
Still the waves with heaven's song
Be the anchor of my soul
Help me sing, "It is well"

Here I am, on my knees
Begging Jesus, please, rescue me

Restore the love long lost at sea
Revive Your Spirit inside of me
Be the anchor of my soul
Help me sing, "It is well"

No more ships passing in the night
No more empty kisses "goodnight"
No more prayerless loveless days
No more getting by with just okay
No more fear in the dead of night
No more shadows blocking the light
No more storms inside of me

Please, Jesus, rescue me...

As Sadie's fingers trailed across the black and white keys, ending back where they began on middle C, her phone rang. An uncontrollable smile spread across her face as she appreciated the familiar scrawl of lyrics and chords across the envelope. 'Hello, this is Sadie.'

'Mrs Patel, it's Dr Robinson. Your husband is awake...'

Chapter 9

'Hey...' Sadie leaned in and gently kissed Vaishant. 'How are you feeling?'

He groaned as he adjusted himself in the bed. 'Better now.'

'Just take it easy.'

'We've been telling him,' the nurse said with a grin. 'But when he found out his wife was here, he just about tried to walk out.'

Sadie shook her head and took his hand. 'What am I going to do with you?'

'I'm sorry,' Vaishant began, 'the accident...'

'It wasn't your fault. And Nyssie is fine, so don't worry.'

He attempted a smile. 'You're...'

'Different?' she offered.

'No... you're *back*.'

She held back her tears, trying to focus on her gratitude over anything else. She nodded slowly. 'Yeah... I'm back... it seems I just needed a bit of a wake-up call.'

'Sorry it was so dramatic.'

She laughed and cried at once. 'Just don't do it again, okay?'

He nodded.

She leaned in and pressed her forehead gently to his. 'Never again.'

She lingered there, grateful to be breathing the same air as her husband. Wishing she could curl up against him like she used to.

'Careful,' he whispered.

'Am I hurting you?'

A half-smile crept across his mouth. 'No... careful I don't drag you up on here.'

The nurse swiftly turned with her clipboard, 'I can do his obs later,' she said. 'Blood pressure may be a little high at the moment, anyway.'

Vaishant chuckled then groaned in pain.

'Oh...' Sadie tried to draw back but he took her arm.

'Don't you dare,' he said. 'I'm never letting you go again.'

'Look at this,' she said softly, showing him the envelope.

'Is that what I think it is?'

She nodded.

'You defacing my property?'

She giggled. 'It's a song.'

'Mmm, that's good.'

As he began to drift off again, Sadie kissed his bandaged head. 'I love you.'

'Mmm...'

Sadie dragged herself away from the hospital and drove back to the shack. For the first time in a long time, hope filled her. Joy was stronger than fear. Gratitude stronger than any hardship.

Nyssa's smile when she saw her mummy was priceless and Sadie carried her over to the window to see the new growth on their stem – she would have to tell Vaishant about it tomorrow. That was when she noticed the strangers in her backyard. Her stomach dropped and her arms instinctively tightened around Nyssa. '*What... who...*'

'It's okay,' Ally quickly said.

Then Sadie recognised Jo. 'What is *she* doing here?'

'The team heard about the accident.' Ally shrugged. 'Apparently, this was what they wanted to do. Plant a garden for your family.'

Tears stung Sadie's eyes. '*What?*'

'Vaishant is already a valued member of their team. Jo came by this morning with everyone and I couldn't think of a logical reason to send them away. I mean, look, it's already less of a jungle out there.'

Sadie couldn't control the tears now rolling down her face. 'We've never had a proper garden. Vaishant has always wanted one. But we've always lived in apartments and...' Sadie swallowed hard. 'I'll be back in a moment.'

Carrying Nyssa, Sadie ventured to the backyard where at least ten capable bodies ripped weeds and dead shrubs while others carried fresh ferns and plants and bags of fertiliser.

'Sadie!' Jo instantly took off her gloves and walked over. 'I hope this is okay, we wanted to help in some way, and this is the only way we really know how, to be honest. How is Vaishant?'

'Awake.' Sadie smiled. 'This is Nyssie... You didn't get to meet properly the other day.'

Jo flashed her bright smile. 'That's right, we didn't. Hey Nyssie... your daddy talks about you and your beautiful mummy all day.'

Sadie's stomach knotted and flipped.

'She's so precious, Sadie,' Jo said, her eyes misty. 'You must be so proud.'

Sadie cleared her throat. 'Would you like a cuddle?'

'Me? I'm a bit dirty...'

'She'll be okay,' Sadie said, leaning in.

Nyssie went to her, reaching to play with Jo's ponytail.

'She likes you.'

Jo gazed at Nyssa. 'Oh, enjoy her, Sadie. She's so precious...'

Sadie watched Jo for a long moment, trying to discern whether she was going to laugh or cringe when Nyssa yanked her hair.

Jo smiled a bittersweet smile. 'My husband and I can't have children.'

Sadie wanted to say she looked too young to be married or to be having children. She wanted to assure her it was hard work and at least this way she could give them back. But then, she knew a deeper truth. She would never trade this life for anything. Despite the anxiety and postpartum depression, Sadie wouldn't go back and do anything differently. Except, perhaps, appreciate what she had sooner.

'I'm so sorry,' Sadie said, acknowledging the fact for what it was – something that deserved grieving. 'That must be hard.'

'Thank you,' Jo said softly, easing Nyssa back into her mother's arms. 'You're very blessed.'

Those words stayed with Sadie for the rest of the day and even once Ally, Jo and "the team" went home for the day, the words still remained. *You're very blessed.*

After bath time, once Nyssa was asleep, Sadie called the hospital to say goodnight to Vaishant.

'Are you okay in the house by yourself?' he asked.

She hadn't given it much thought. 'Yeah, I'm okay. I'm looking forward to you coming home though.'

'Me too.'

Chapter 10

The following weekend, Vaishant was cleared to go home and, if he took it easy, to church on the Sunday. After enjoying a morning in the garden, they walked down Sadie's usual route to the community centre. There was a casual warmth, which they hadn't experienced at other churches. The congregants sat at café tables; the worship team was nothing more than an acoustic guitar and a couple of singers. And when the pastor stood up to speak, he still had his take-away coffee in hand. Still, Jesus was in this place. The stripped back songs left room for the Spirit alone to move hearts and Sadie's wasn't the only tear-stained face. Something had shifted in her. She committed to reading her Bible everyday, she spent her afternoons talking through life with Ally, and Nyssa was sleeping better with her fresh air naps. And then there was Vaishant. Yesterday he had been tired when he got home. But this morning he seemed more himself, as though their gift of a garden was restoring him. She could feel him drawing closer to her. A hand on her knee that she didn't flinch away from. A kiss on the hair or just a knowing look. It made her strangely nervous – in the best way.

As they walked home from the community centre, Sadie's heart was full. She would look over at her husband, smile, then keep walking.

His eyes glinted.

'I like it when you look at me like that,' she said lightly. 'I thought for a while there you might not want me anymore.'

He stopped mid-step. 'What do you mean?'

'I just thought since the pregnancy or the labour and my body changing, you might not want me anymore. But it's nice, you're looking at me the way you used to.'

Vaishant's eyes only grew wider. 'You really thought that?'

She nodded and went to push the stroller. But he took hold of the handle.

'Why didn't you say something sooner?'

'We've both been so tired. And you've been working so hard... there has just never been a right time...'

Clouds shifted and he squinted against the sunlight as the dirt road changed from overcast to full sun. 'You thought I didn't want you because your body changed carrying and giving birth to our beautiful daughter?' He challenged, gesturing to a sleeping Nyssa. 'You thought I didn't want you because I saw your incredible strength in that delivery room?' He took a step toward her and added softly, 'You thought I wouldn't want you because your body is more curvaceous now?'

'And striped,' she said, shifting beneath his gaze.

He cupped her face in his hands. 'Is that what you really thought?'

She opened her mouth to reply but his hands drew her to him. His lips were on hers in an unfamiliar way. There was conviction in his kiss, as though he was trying to prove a point. A new passion ignited, sparked by years of love and a renewed decision to keep loving. When he finally released her, her head spun.

'Believe me?' he asked, breathless.

She nodded. It was all she could do.

But she knew that night Nyssa would sleep in her own cot.

Chapter 11

Sadie woke rested and relaxed. She took the time to make a pot of coffee while Nyssa slept, and then sat down at the dining table for her few precious moments with God.

She cracked her Bible open just as Vaishant's phone pinged. She tried to ignore it, but it pinged again. She briefly wondered why he had left it in the kitchen at all and figured she should see if it was something important.

First was a missed call and voicemail from an international number. The next was one from a mobile number not saved to his phone. Next, a text message written in another language. She swiftly carried the phone to the bedroom and nudged him awake. She stroked his bare broad shoulders. 'You have missed calls.'

He groaned, squinting at the phone. Then he was upright, rereading the message. He hit a button and put the phone to his ear.

'What is it?' Sadie asked.

Once someone answered, he began to speak rapid Hindi.

Sadie tried to keep up but she had never got her head around the language.

Vaishant threw back the quilt as he finished the call. He then threw his phone on the bed and clutched his head with both hands.

'It's my Paapa,' he said softly. 'He died of a heart attack.'

'I'm so sorry.' Sadie wrapped her arms around her husband and buried her face in his chest. He curled around her, holding her close.

Vaishant released a heavy breath. 'My poor Mam...'

Sadie rested her cheek on his chest, listening to the steady beat of his heart. 'You should go.'

'No,' he said softly. 'I have responsibilities here.'

'You don't return to work for another week. It's okay, Nyssie and I will be okay.'

He kissed her hair. 'Sadie... I'm not leaving you. That's all there is to it.'

'Then we should all go.'

His Adams apple bounced in his throat as he gazed down at her. 'You would do that? You've already upended your life for me.'

'Me? You started it,' Sadie breathed. 'You left your family for me. It's the least I can do for them.'

'I'm not leaving,' Vaishant said. 'And I'm not dragging my family to the other side of the world.'

'But they are your family too,' Sadie said gently.

'It's complicated.' And with that, Vaishant went to check on Nyssa.

Sadie's mind raced. Just yesterday she felt so content. Now she didn't know how to feel. Would Vaishant resent her and Nyssa for not having the freedom to visit his family at this tragic time?

'I just don't know what to do,' she confessed to Ally later that day.

'So, Vaishant doesn't want to go?' she asked, keeping her gaze to the ocean beyond.

'He says it's complicated but I don't see why. His father died. His family will need him.'

'Has he had anything to do with his family lately?'

'Not much since we got married. But we haven't been married that long and we've been busy, and I was so sick while pregnant...'

'So, they don't know about Nyssa?'

Sadie thought about it for a moment. 'Well, I'm sure they know about her...'

Ally sipped her coffee. 'So how did they feel about him moving countries to be with you?'

'Like any parent, I suppose.' Sadie shrugged. 'They weren't happy about it, but they accepted it.'

Ally slowly nodded. 'Accepted it or blessed it?'

Sadie stared at her. 'What do you mean?'

'Look, I don't know much about his culture, but it could in fact *be* complicated. It could be something neither of us really understand. Are his family Christian?'

'No,' Sadie replied softly, retrieving her chocolate brownie from its brown paper bag. 'No, they're not.'

'That alone is complicated. I'm guessing their Hindu or Muslim?'

'We... we don't really talk about it to be honest. When we met, he was so intrigued with me and my mum and the work she was doing, he wanted to know what we believed. Then he started to believe it too. We left before he could really tell us what his family thought about it.'

'Maybe it's time to open up the conversation, especially if it's making you anxious again.'

'How did you know it's making me anxious again?'

'Well, it's all we've talked about for the last half hour...'

Sadie didn't know how to bring it up with Vaishant. So, she didn't. The following day she didn't even walk down to the community centre but made an excuse about Nyssa being restless. Which she was. It hadn't been an outright lie. But by the time witching hour arrived, Sadie had her forehead pressed once again to the doorframe, willing Vaishant to come inside. He had been in their garden all afternoon.

Daylight turned to dusk and Sadie fed Nyssa one of her mashed vegetable concoctions before running the bath. She swirled her fingers around in the water to test the temperature. Then she climbed in with Nyssa, ready to wash off the day.

Sadie heard the backdoor close and Vaishant walked into the bathroom, Bible still under his arm.

Nyssa giggled at him, and it softened his expression.

'I've been praying,' he said simply.

The last time he said those words in that same solemn way after seeking the Lord, they up and moved for this new job.

'Okay...'

'Nothing has changed,' he said. 'I still don't believe it's right to go.'

'Okay.'

'It's complicated.'

'Okay,' Sadie replied, for now. But once Nyssa was safely tucked up in her cot, Sadie poured them both a glass of wine and pulled her husband onto the couch.

'I may or may not have given her Panadol to help her sleep,' Sadie confessed.

Vaishant's solemn face broke into a smile. 'Well, she is teething. I don't think that's considered drugging your child.'

Sadie shrugged. 'She'll be okay. But will *we*? Are you going to regret this?'

All amusement left Vaishant's face. 'Is that what has been bothering you?'

'Can you blame me? I took you away from your family and now I feel like it's us stopping you from grieving with them.'

He released a heavy sigh. 'My parents told me that if I moved here and married you that I would no longer be their son.'

Sadie stared at her husband with simultaneous horror and admiration. 'What?'

'It was bad enough I was a Christian, but they accepted it because of the financial aid we received from your mother. The chain of poverty was broken with me because of your mother's generosity.'

Sadie swallowed hard. 'So, is that why you married me? In gratitude to my mother.'

'You can't be serious,' he said softly.

'Just answer the question.'

He took both her hands in his own. 'Aren't you listening to anything I'm saying? I left my family because I was – *am* – completely in love with you. Their ultimatum was a mistake because I didn't even hesitate. I knew what I wanted. What I *still* want. And it's you. Our family. This is my family. You and Nyssie. A man leaves his father and mother and becomes one with his wife. You are part of me, Sadie. And if they do not accept you, then they do not accept me either.'

'Isn't it hard though, holding onto all these feelings?'

'But I don't.' He shrugged. 'I give them to Jesus. Today I wanted to make sure it wasn't bitterness that was stopping me from returning but God gave me complete peace about it. I will send them a letter and some financial aid for the funeral. But my brother made it clear, my mother doesn't even want me at the funeral. Though he thought the decision should still be mine.'

'Shan, I'm so sorry.'

'Don't be.' He kissed her hands. 'I would not trade our lives for anything. I'm so grateful for you and Nyssie. You are a blessing from God.'

Sadie leaned forward and kissed him. 'I love you,' she breathed.

How can I thank You
For all that You are
And all I cannot see

How can I praise You
Words aren't enough
So my soul must sing

How can I know You
More every day
Lord, help my unbelief

Chapter 12

Vaishant slowly returned to work, which made the weekends all the more precious and Sunday mornings all the more praise worthy – particularly when a local donated their upright piano. Sadie finally could play again in worship while Vaishant held Nyssa with one arm and raised his other to heaven. Sadie would leave the humble service at the community centre each week with a full heart, equipped for the week ahead. She felt strong for the first time in a long time. As though the storm that had been raging within her for the past year or so had finally calmed.

Ally had warned her though – *the days may be long but the years go so quickly*. It proved true. Soon they were celebrating Nyssa's first birthday in the shack's backyard and Sadie's orchid joined the occasion with its single full bloom.

'Do you need a hand with anything?' Jo asked as she squeezed into the kitchen bursting with treats sourced from the community centre's baker.

'You don't look like you should be lifting a finger,' Ally told her.

Sadie glanced up from arranging the cupcake tray. 'She's right, Jo. You don't look so well. Are you okay?'

It was a question that opened the floodgates.

Tears fell freely as Jo's face twisted. 'I'm pregnant...'

Sadie and Ally looked at each other then back to Jo. The cupcakes could wait. Taking Jo by the hand, Sadie led her to the couch where she and Vaishant had had many heart to hearts. It was a safe space. She hoped Jo would feel it too.

'I'm ten weeks pregnant,' she went on softly. 'And I'm terrified. I'm so happy. But so scared of losing the baby.'

'Oh sweetheart.' Ally took hold of her free hand.

'It's a pure miracle,' Jo said. 'We were told we would never conceive naturally. We had given up... and then... I'm so sorry to do this today. On Nyssie's birthday and...'

'Oh, she won't remember,' Sadie said, trying to lighten the mood. 'Is this why you've reduced your hours at work?'

Jo nodded. 'I'm so scared that I'll do something to hurt the baby.'

'Have you told Shan?'

Jo shook her head.

'Do you mind if I tell him? Maybe it would be good for someone to look out for you. Do any heavy lifting, no questions asked?'

'I'm the manager,' she said helplessly. 'I'm the one who is meant to lead by example.'

'In a few weeks, everyone will know the reason you're taking it easy,' Ally said. 'You won't be able to hide it forever.'

Jo smiled through her tears.

'And in the meantime, why don't you meet us at the beach on your free afternoons?' Sadie offered. 'We just sit and chat, drink coffee...'

'I can do decaf, too.' Ally winked.

'That would be...' Jo started crying again, 'so nice. Thank you.'

'And just remember.' Sadie squeezed her hand. 'God has not given us a spirit of fear, but of power, love and a sound mind. That became my mantra when I was going through postpartum anxiety and depression.'

Jo's brow creased. 'Oh, I'm sorry, I had no idea.'

'Well, let's just say, I know what it's like to be terrified. But I also know what it's like to be on the other side of that fear. And it's only Jesus that leads us there. And honesty. Admitting where you're at isn't where you want to be is one of the bravest things you can do.'

Vaishant appeared in the doorway. 'Uh... sorry to interrupt,' he began awkwardly. 'Nyssie is allowed to eat cake now, right? Because... she is.'

Sadie smiled. 'If she can't on her birthday, then when can she?'

When Sadie met with Ally and Jo that Monday afternoon for coffee and chocolate brownies, Ally pulled out her well-loved Bible.

'I thought we could start here. Then have a time of prayer.'

Sadie gazed over at the still blue ocean as Ally read from the book of Psalms. Nyssa had given up sleeping in the stroller but played happily beside them, picking daisies and plucking their petals as though playing "He loves me, he loves me not".

Oh, He loves you, alright, Sadie thought. *Even more than I do. And that's a lot...* Sadie smoothed Nyssa's dark downy hair then kissed it.

'*The Lord sits enthroned over the flood; the Lord is enthroned as King forever,*' Ally read aloud. '*The Lord gives strength to his people; the Lord blesses his people with peace.*'

About the Author

Elizabeth Chapman is a writer journeying with Jesus. She has a Graduate Diploma in Creative Writing and is studying a Master of Divinity.

As the founder of Daughters of Love & Light, Elizabeth is passionate about creativity and calling.

She's a full-time Mum living in South Australia with her husband, young son, and three cats, and often writes in stolen moments.

www.ingramcontent.com/pod-product-compliance
Lightning Source LLC
Chambersburg PA
CBHW070400120726
47909CB00008B/2924